MW00973823

To my beautiful daughters, Elizabeth and Stephanie, who have taken turns testing out their wings and flying from the nest. Thanks for your encouragement and support.

To my four new and beautiful nieces: Mikaylee, Ariella, Kiara, and Ashlyn. May you always remember that God made you special.

Special thanks to my editors, Mary Jo Zazueta and Laura Vasile, and to all the dedicated people who helped me see this book to completion.

www.mascotbooks.com

For more information, please contact:
Mascot Books
560 Herndon Parkway #120
Herndon, VA 20170
info@mascotbooks.com

Library of Congress Control Number: 2012952668

CPSIA Code: PRT1112A
ISBN: 1620861526
ISBN-13: 9781620861523

Printed in the United States

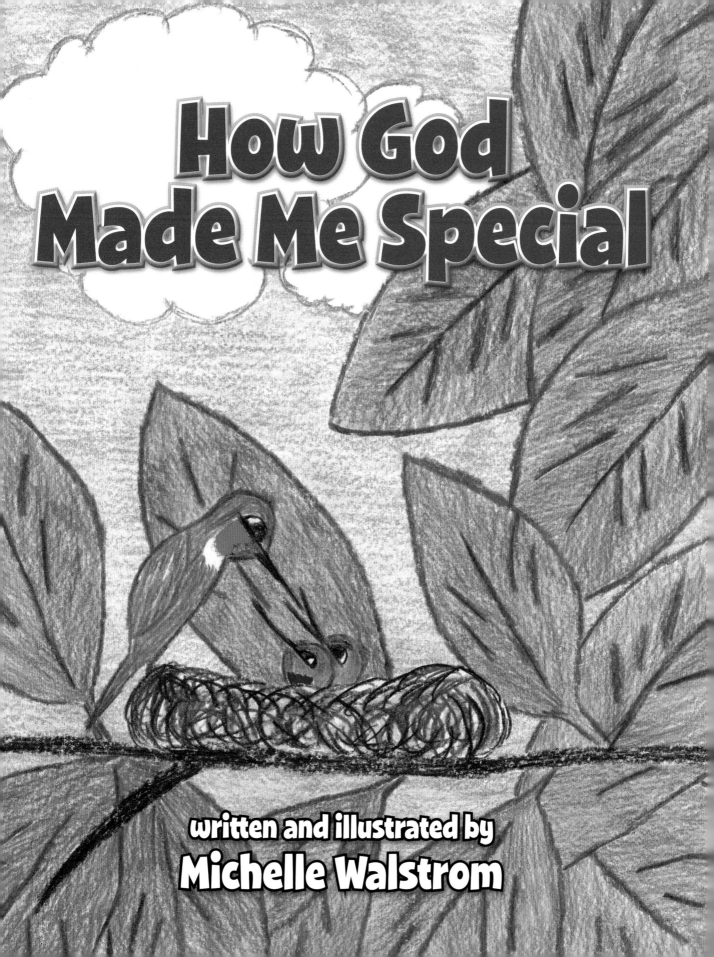

How God Made Me Special

written and illustrated by
Michelle Walstrom

One chilly summer night, I hatched out of a tiny eggshell.

As my mother covered my brother and I with her large, warm wing, she said, "God made you special."

I was too little to ask, but I wondered how God had made me special.

Nine days later, our eyes opened and we saw our beautiful mother as she fed us nectar. She looked down at us and said, "God made you special."

I swallowed my nectar as fast as I could and used all of my strength to quietly chirp, "Why?"

To my surprise, Mama heard me and answered, "God has given you brilliant eyesight so you can enjoy seeing all of his creations."

We peeked out of the nest and looked around. Our mama was right. God had given us eyes to see the grass on the hills, the leaves on the trees, and the beautiful wildflowers.

The next morning as we woke up, Mama said, "God made you special."

"Because I can see?" my brother asked confidently.

"Yes. But in a couple weeks, when you are fully grown, you will also be able to fly. You will fly forward, backward, in place, and even upside down."

"That sounds like fun!" we said with excitement.

The next day, when our mama was grooming us, she said, "God made you special."

"Because I can see and soon fly?" I happily asked.

"Yes. But you can hear very well, too. Listen. What do you hear?" Mama asked.

We listened carefully. We heard the water as it fell from a waterfall and the wind as it blew through the leaves on our tree. We heard a bumblebee as it gathered pollen from a flower. We even heard human children playing down the street.

As I listened to the wonderful sounds, I said, "God made us special."

The next day, as Mama repaired our nest after a storm the previous night, she said, "God made you special."

"Because we can see, hear, and soon fly?" asked my brother. We both hoped Mama would tell us something new.

"Yes. But we are hummingbirds, the tiniest birds in the whole world," Mama said.

My brother and I watched the other birds that lived near us. That night, I said, "You're right, Mama. We are the tiniest birds! God made us special."

The next day, Mama brought my brother and I our first tiny bug to eat. "God made you special," she said.

We couldn't wait to hear what else made us special. I quickly said, "God made us special because we can see brilliantly and soon we will be able to fly like no other birds. We can hear very well. We are hummingbirds, the smallest birds in the whole world. How else has God made us special?"

"Well, my dears, you are also very smart. You will be able to remember every flower from which you have eaten. You will also know how long it will take before that flower will provide food for you again."

Every day, Mama told us how special we were. She made sure we knew how to survive once we left our wonderful nest.

Time flew by quickly and one day, with a tear in her eye, Mama said, "God made you special, and now it is time for both of you to make nests of your own."

I was scared and excited all at the same time. I hugged Mama when she said we could visit anytime.

As we flew from the nest, Mama yelled out, "Remember, God made you special!"

I practiced flying backward, and flew back to Mama. I hugged her once more and told her, "Remember, Mama, God made you special, too."

The End

<u>Note to the reader</u>

Dear reader,

    Can you imagine how special you are to God? If God took the time to make each one of his animal creations special, imagine how much more you mean to Him.

    When God created the animals, He said, "It was good." But when God created Adam, the first human, He said, "It was very good."

    Just think: there is no one else in the world exactly like you. God made you special and wants to be your personal friend. Every day, whether you are happy or sad, remember that God loves you and He made you special.

With love,

Michelle Walstrom

For more information about the author,

please check out her website:

michellewalstrom.com